THE MAN IN THE IRON MASK

Vol. 4: The Man in the Iron Mask
Adapted from the novel by ALEXANDRE DUMAS

THE STORY SO FAR:

In the 17th century, **Athos**, **Porthos**, and **Aramis**—famed as "The Three Musketeers"—were joined in friendship by young **d'Artagnan**, in service to King Louis XIII of France. Three decades later, Athos had become a count—Porthos, by marriage, a baron—and shrewd Aramis, the Bishop of Vannes. D'Artagnan now commanded the Musketeers.

Aramis learned that **Philippe**, a prisoner in the Bastille, was in fact the twin brother of **King Louis XIV**, held in seclusion since birth, lest knowledge of his existence lead to civil war. Aramis devised a conspiracy to put Louis in prison and Philippe upon the throne, with the unwitting help of Porthos and of **Nicholas Fouquet**, the nation's Surintendant (chief tax collector).

But the scheme failed, because, when Fouquet learned of it, he freed Louis. Philippe was sentenced to be forever imprisoned on an island, wearing an iron mask so no one could ever again view his resemblance to the King. Fouquet had given Aramis and Porthos four hours' head start to ride into exile on the fortress estate of Belle-Isle, off the coast....

Writer **Roy Thomas**	Special Thanks **Deborah Sherer & Freeman Henry**	Penciler **Hugo Petrus**	Inker **Tom Palmer**
Colorist **June Chung**	Letterer **Virtual Calligraphy's Joe Caramagna**	Cover **Marko Djurdjevic**	Special Thanks **Chris Allo**	Production **Anthony Dial**
Assistant Editor **Lauren Sankovitch**	Associate Editor **Nicole Boose**	Editor **Ralph Macchio**	Editor in Chief **Joe Quesada**	Publisher **Dan Buckley**

VISIT US AT
www.abdopublishing.com

Reinforced library bound edition published in 2009 by Spotlight, a division of the ABDO Group, 8000 West 78th Street, Edina, Minnesota 55439. Spotlight produces high-quality reinforced library bound editions for schools and libraries. Published by agreement with Marvel Characters, Inc.

Library of Congress Cataloging-in-Publication Data

Thomas, Roy, 1940-
    The man in the iron mask / adapted from the novel by Alexandre Dumas ; Roy Thomas, writer ; Hugo Petrus, penciler ; Tom Palmer, inker ; Virtual Calligraphy's Joe Caramagna, letterer ; June Chung, colorist. -- Reinforced library bound ed.
       v. cm.
     "Marvel."
    Contents: v. 1. The three musketeers -- v. 2. High treason -- v. 3. The iron mask -- v. 4. The man in the iron mask -- v. 5. The death of a titan -- v. 6. Musketeers no more.
    ISBN 9781599615943 (v. 1) -- ISBN 9781599615950 (v. 2) -- ISBN 9781599615967 (v. 3) -- ISBN 9781599615974 (v. 4) -- ISBN 9781599615981 (v. 5) -- ISBN 9781599615998 (v. 6)
    Summary: Retells, in comic book format, Alexandre Dumas' tale of political intrigue, romance, and adventure in seventeenth-century France.
    [1. Dumas, Alexandre, 1802-1870.--Adaptations. 2. Graphic novels. 3. Adventure and adventurers--Fiction. 4. France--History--Louis XIII, 1610-1643--Fiction.] I. Dumas, Alexandre, 1802-1870. II. Petrus, Hugo. VI. Title.
PZ7.7.T518 Man 2009
[Fic]--dc22   2008035321

All Spotlight books have reinforced library bindings and are manufactured in the United States of America.

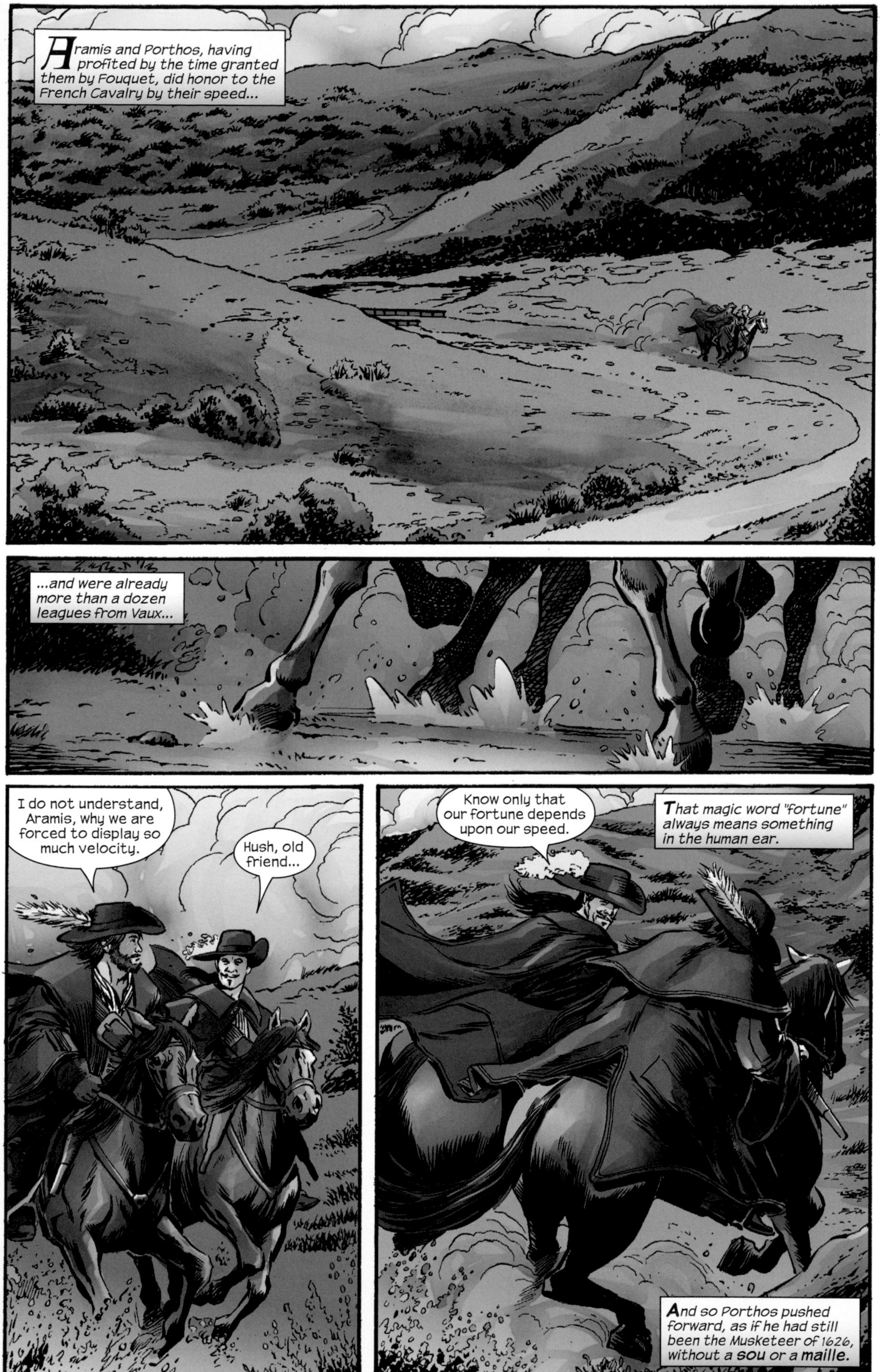
Aramis and Porthos, having profited by the time granted them by Fouquet, did honor to the French Cavalry by their speed...
...and were already more than a dozen leagues from Vaux...
I do not understand, Aramis, why we are forced to display so much velocity.
Hush, old friend...
Know only that our fortune depends upon our speed.
That magic word "fortune" always means something in the human ear.
And so Porthos pushed forward, as if he had still been the Musketeer of 1626, without a sou or a maille.

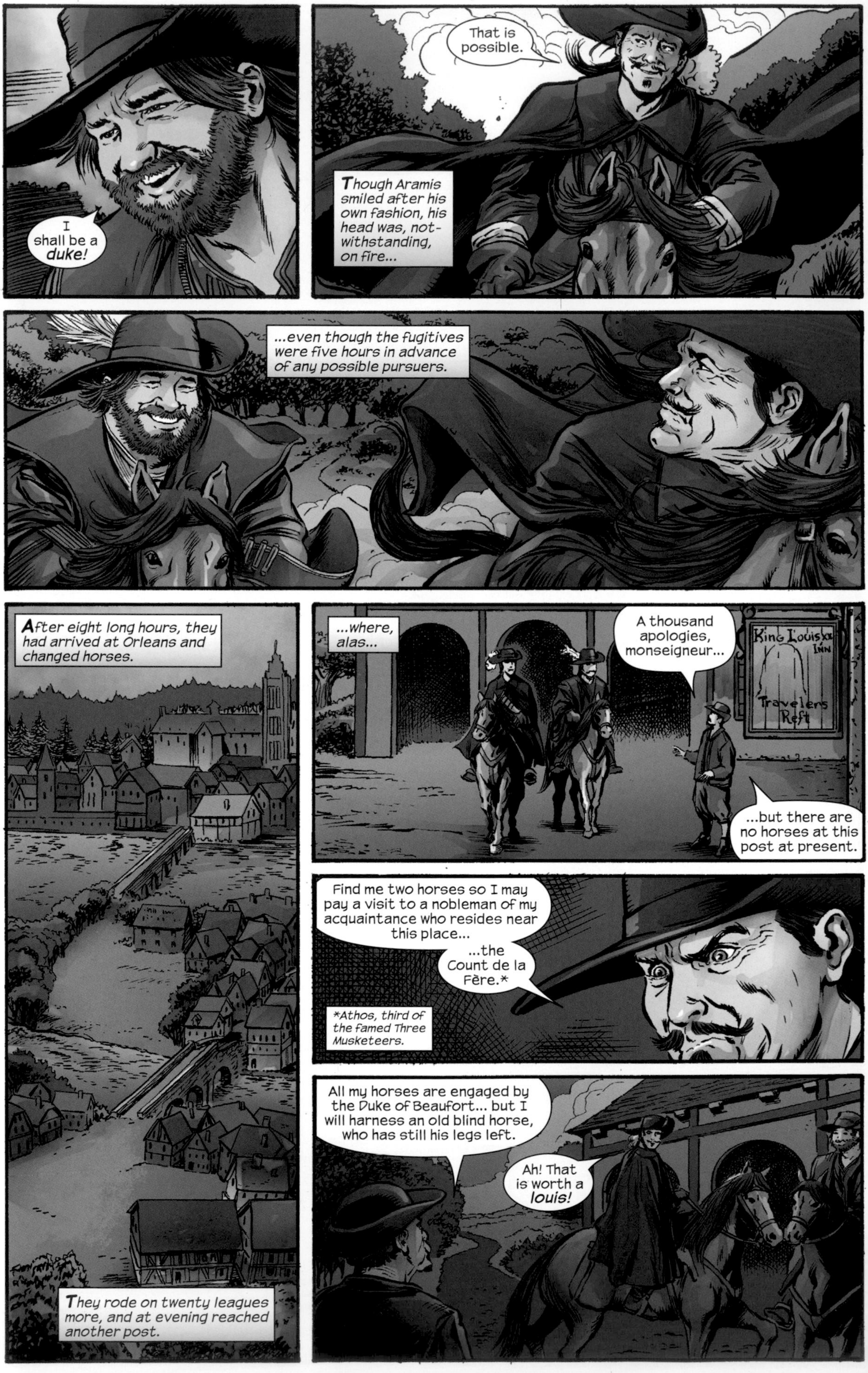

I shall be a *duke!*
That is possible.
Though Aramis smiled after his own fashion, his head was, notwithstanding, on fire...
...even though the fugitives were five hours in advance of any possible pursuers.
After eight long hours, they had arrived at Orleans and changed horses.
They rode on twenty leagues more, and at evening reached another post.
...where, alas...
A thousand apologies, monseigneur...
King Louis XI INN
Travelers Rest
...but there are no horses at this post at present.
Find me two horses so I may pay a visit to a nobleman of my acquaintance who resides near this place...
...the Count de la Fère.*
*Athos, third of the famed Three Musketeers.
All my horses are engaged by the Duke of Beaufort... but I will harness an old blind horse, who has still his legs left.
Ah! That is worth a *louis!*

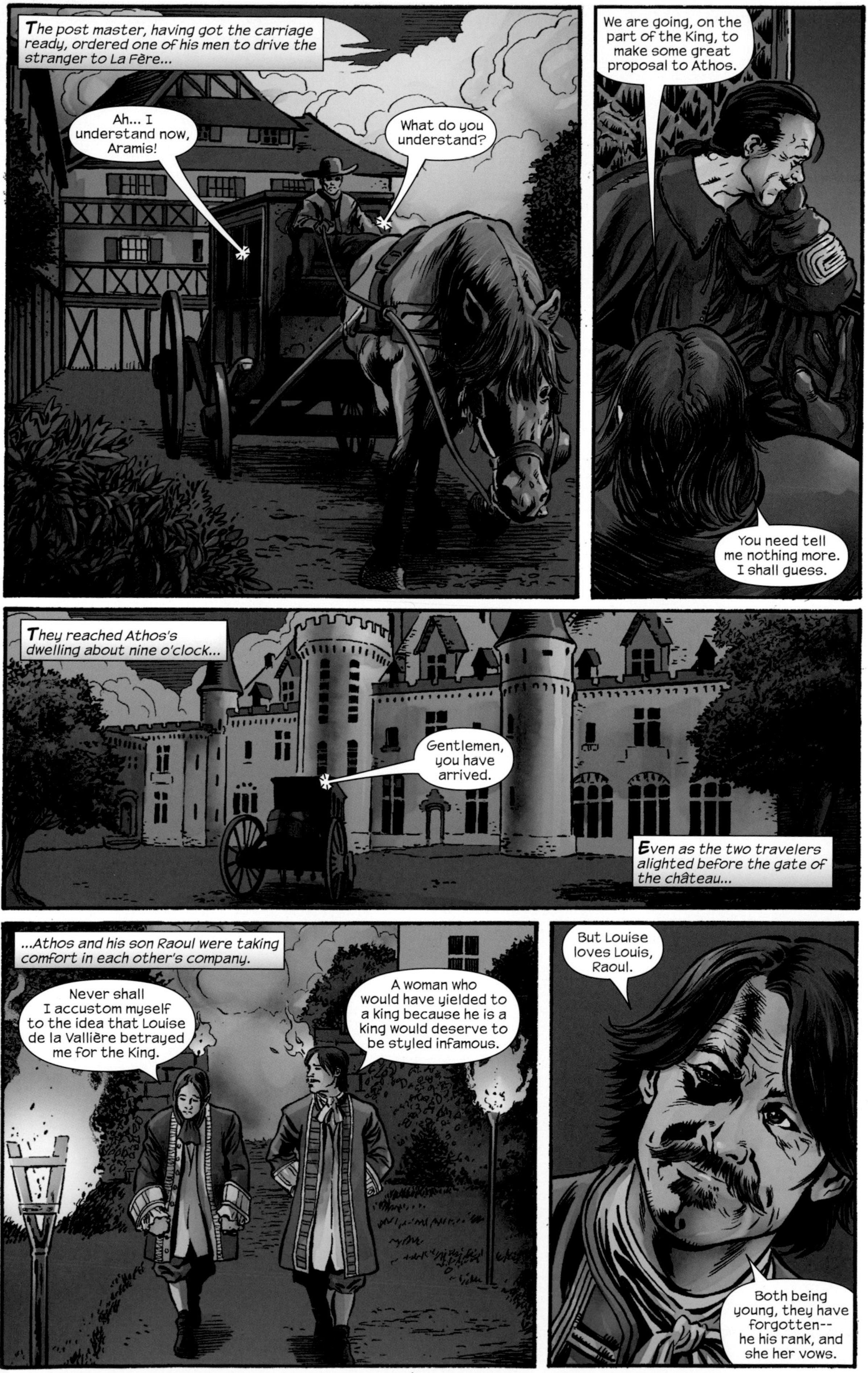
The post master, having got the carriage ready, ordered one of his men to drive the stranger to La Fère...
Ah... I understand now, Aramis!
What do you understand?
We are going, on the part of the King, to make some great proposal to Athos.
You need tell me nothing more. I shall guess.
They reached Athos's dwelling about nine o'clock...
Gentlemen, you have arrived.
Even as the two travelers alighted before the gate of the château...
...Athos and his son Raoul were taking comfort in each other's company.
Never shall I accustom myself to the idea that Louise de la Vallière betrayed me for the King.
A woman who would have yielded to a king because he is a king would deserve to be styled infamous.
But Louise loves Louis, Raoul.
Both being young, they have forgotten-- he his rank, and she her vows.

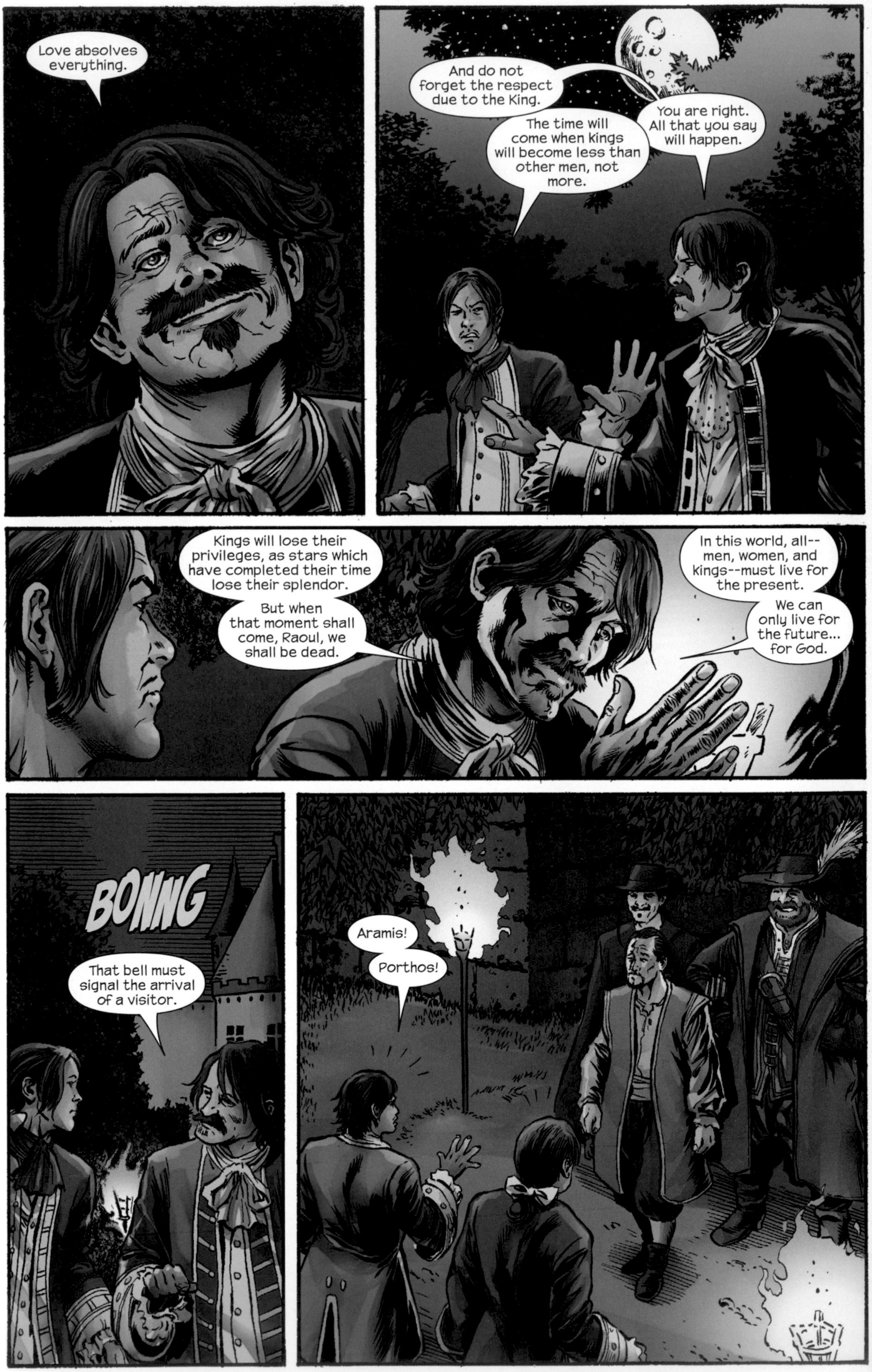
Love absolves everything.
And do not forget the respect due to the King.
The time will come when kings will become less than other men, not more.
You are right. All that you say will happen.
Kings will lose their privileges, as stars which have completed their time lose their splendor.
But when that moment shall come, Raoul, we shall be dead.
In this world, all-- men, women, and kings--must live for the present.
We can only live for the future... for God.
BONNG
That bell must signal the arrival of a visitor.
Aramis!
Porthos!

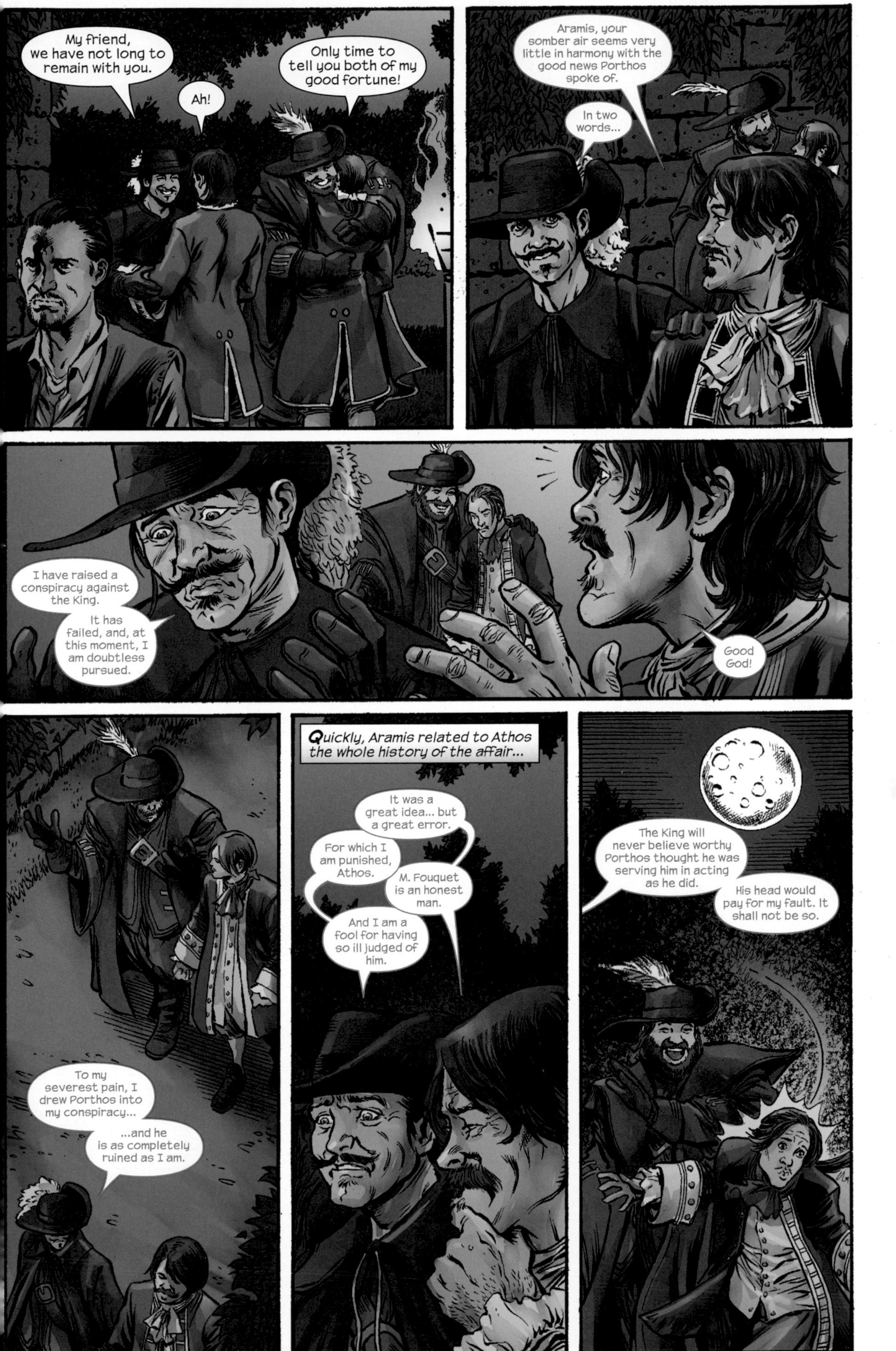

My friend, we have not long to remain with you.
Ah!
Only time to tell you both of my good fortune!
Aramis, your somber air seems very little in harmony with the good news Porthos spoke of.
In two words...
I have raised a conspiracy against the King.
It has failed, and, at this moment, I am doubtless pursued.
Good God!
To my severest pain, I drew Porthos into my conspiracy...
...and he is as completely ruined as I am.
Quickly, Aramis related to Athos the whole history of the affair...
It was a great idea... but a great error.
For which I am punished, Athos.
M. Fouquet is an honest man.
And I am a fool for having so ill judged of him.
The King will never believe worthy Porthos thought he was serving him in acting as he did.
His head would pay for my fault. It shall not be so.

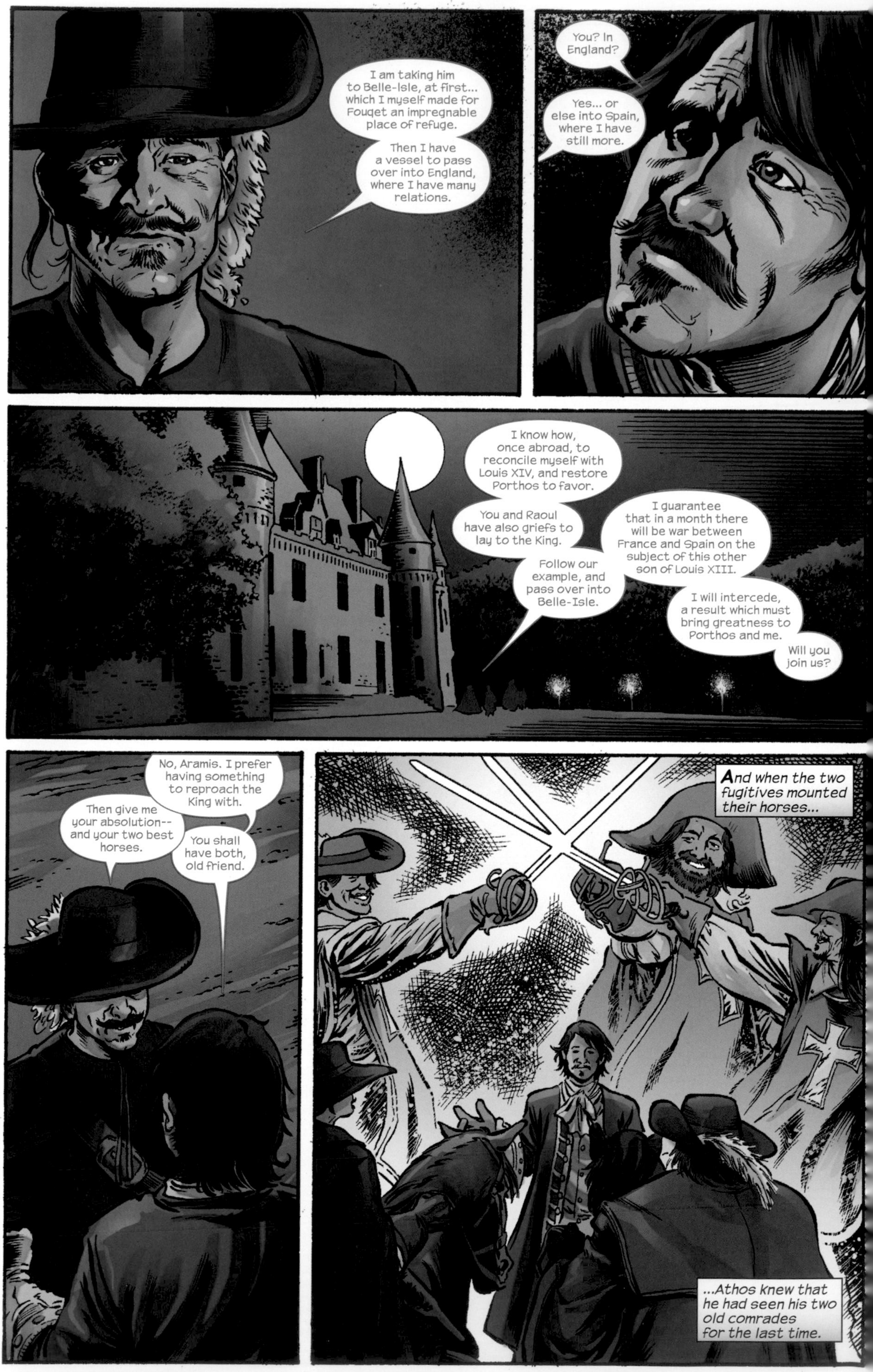
I am taking him to Belle-Isle, at first... which I myself made for Fouqet an impregnable place of refuge.
Then I have a vessel to pass over into England, where I have many relations.
You? In England?
Yes... or else into Spain, where I have still more.
I know how, once abroad, to reconcile myself with Louis XIV, and restore Porthos to favor.
You and Raoul have also griefs to lay to the King.
Follow our example, and pass over into Belle-Isle.
I guarantee that in a month there will be war between France and Spain on the subject of this other son of Louis XIII.
I will intercede, a result which must bring greatness to Porthos and me.
Will you join us?
No, Aramis. I prefer having something to reproach the King with.
Then give me your absolution-- and your two best horses.
You shall have both, old friend.
And when the two fugitives mounted their horses...
...Athos knew that he had seen his two old comrades for the last time.

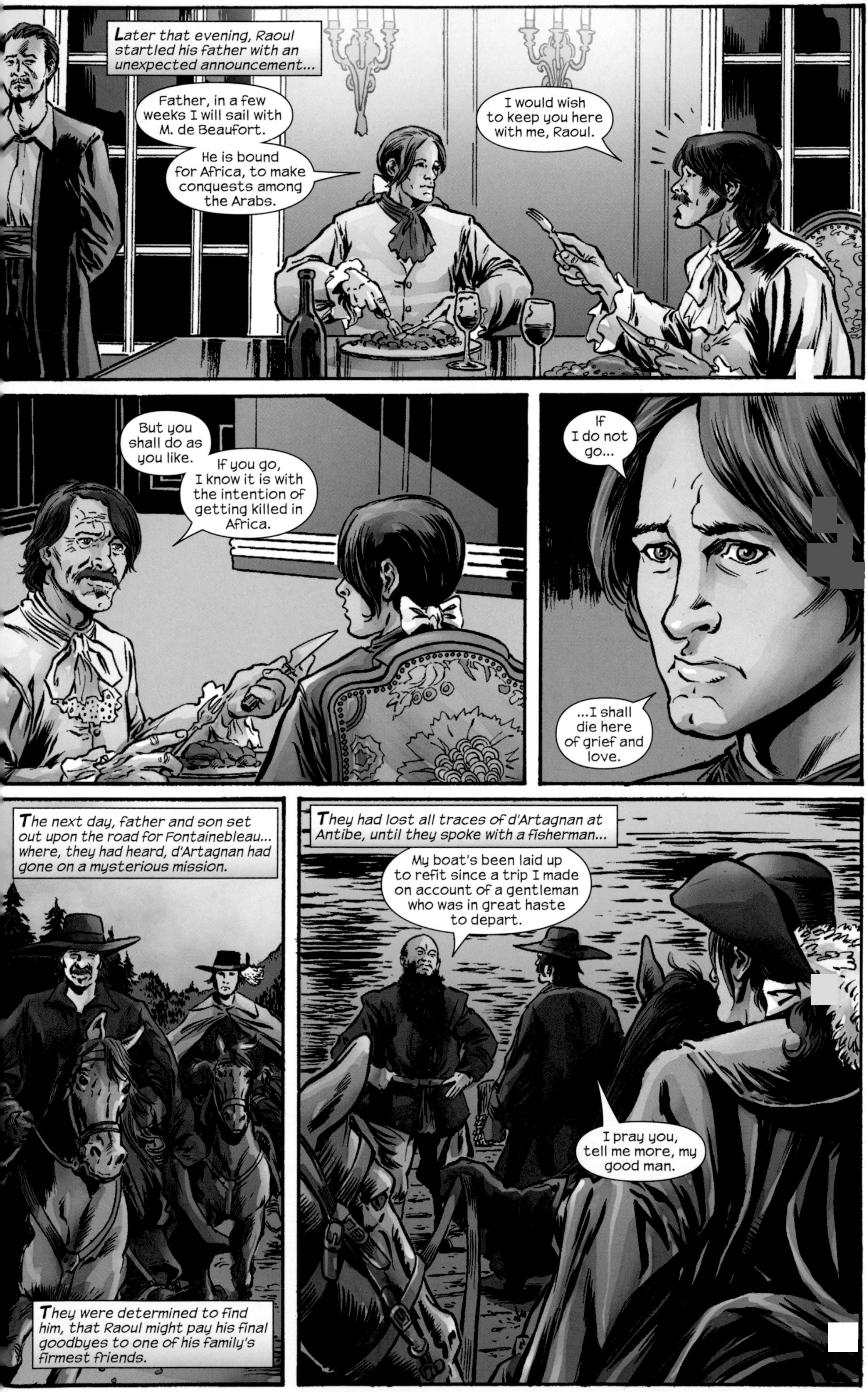
Later that evening, Raoul startled his father with an unexpected announcement...
Father, in a few weeks I will sail with M. de Beaufort.
He is bound for Africa, to make conquests among the Arabs.
I would wish to keep you here with me, Raoul.
But you shall do as you like.
If you go, I know it is with the intention of getting killed in Africa.
If I do not go...
...I shall die here of grief and love.
The next day, father and son set out upon the road for Fontainebleau... where, they had heard, d'Artagnan had gone on a mysterious mission.
They were determined to find him, that Raoul might pay his final goodbyes to one of his family's firmest friends.
They had lost all traces of d'Artagnan at Antibe, until they spoke with a fisherman...
My boat's been laid up to refit since a trip I made on account of a gentleman who was in great haste to depart.
I pray you, tell me more, my good man.

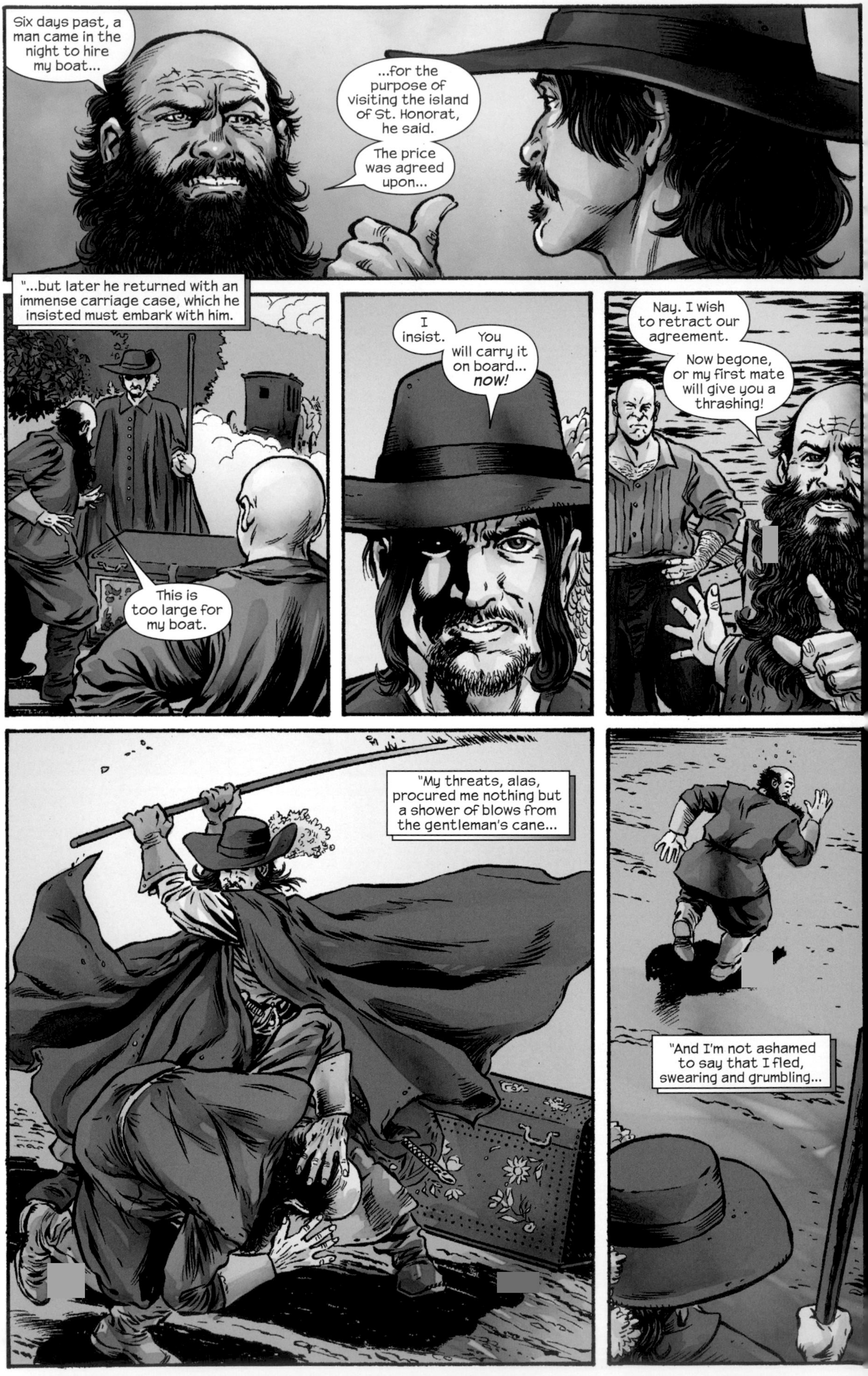
Six days past, a man came in the night to hire my boat...
...for the purpose of visiting the island of St. Honorat, he said.
The price was agreed upon...
"...but later he returned with an immense carriage case, which he insisted must embark with him.
This is too large for my boat.
I insist.
You will carry it on board... *now!*
Nay. I wish to retract our agreement.
Now begone, or my first mate will give you a thrashing!
"My threats, alas, procured me nothing but a shower of blows from the gentleman's cane...
"And I'm not ashamed to say that I fled, swearing and grumbling...

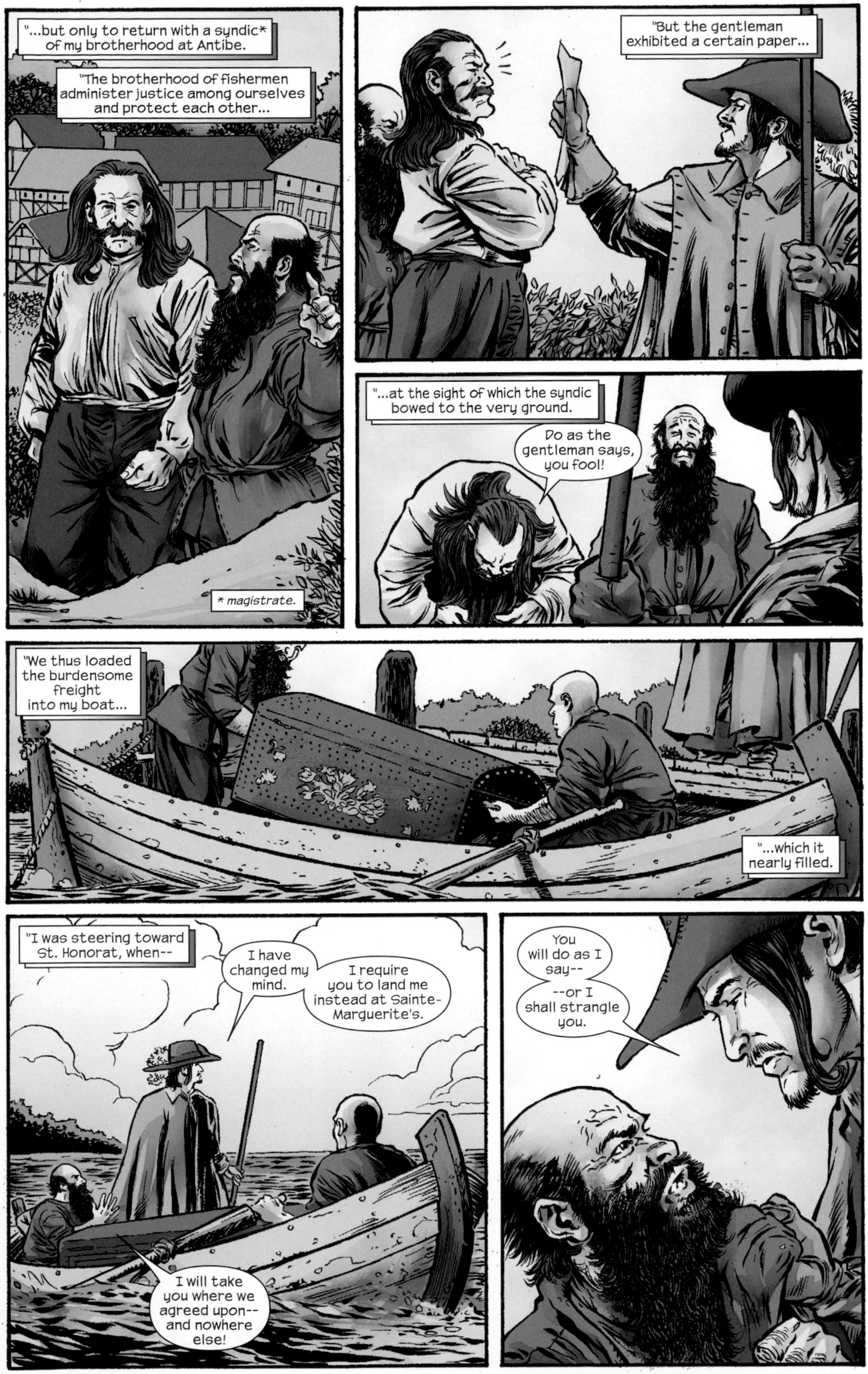
"...but only to return with a syndic* of my brotherhood at Antibe.
"The brotherhood of fishermen administer justice among ourselves and protect each other...
* magistrate.
"But the gentleman exhibited a certain paper...
"...at the sight of which the syndic bowed to the very ground.
Do as the gentleman says, you fool!
"We thus loaded the burdensome freight into my boat...
"...which it nearly filled.
"I was steering toward St. Honorat, when--
I have changed my mind.
I require you to land me instead at Sainte-Marguerite's.
I will take you where we agreed upon--and nowhere else!
You will do as I say--
--or I shall strangle you.

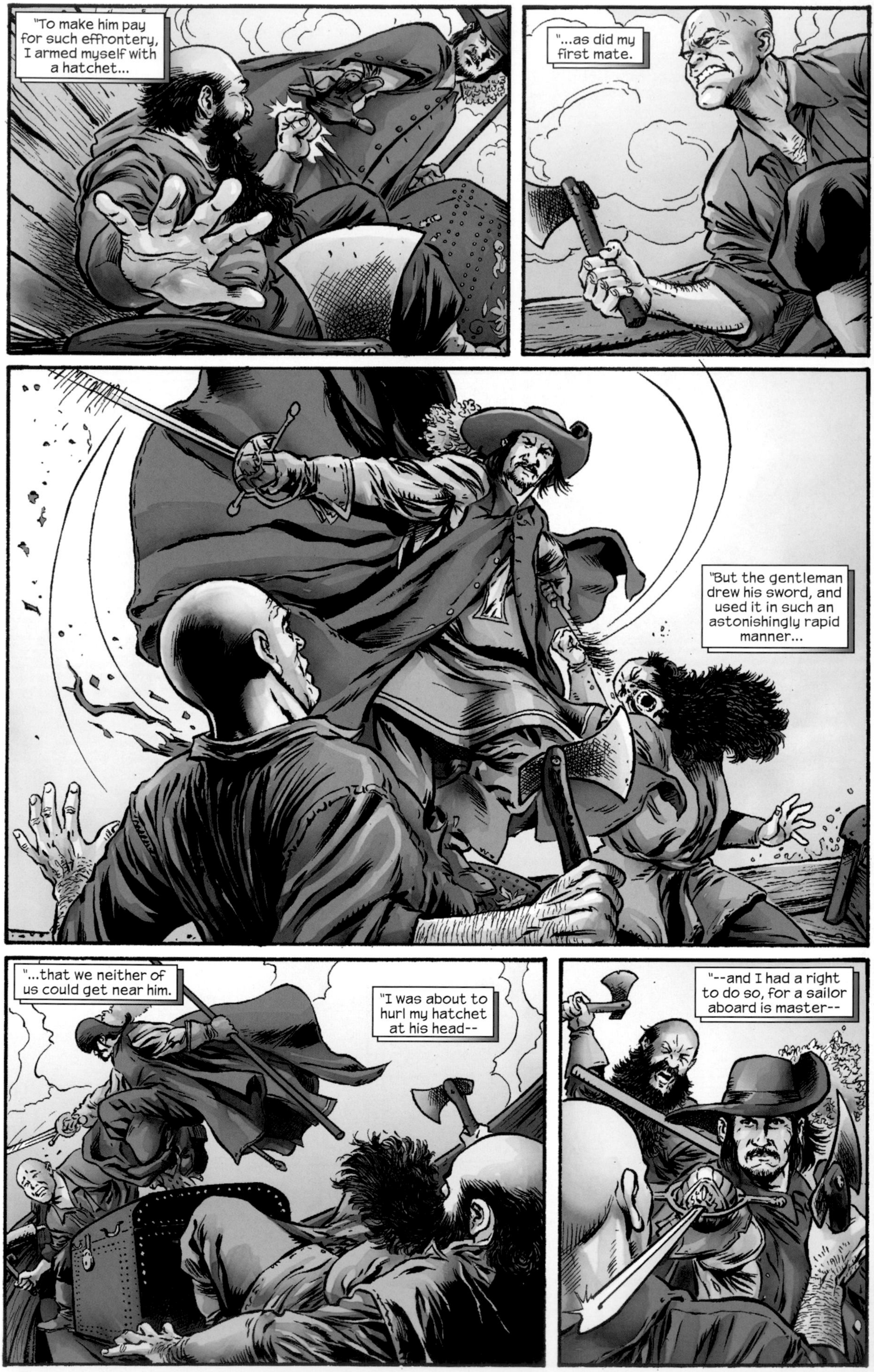
"To make him pay for such effrontery, I armed myself with a hatchet...
"...as did my first mate.
"But the gentleman drew his sword, and used it in such an astonishingly rapid manner...
"...that we neither of us could get near him.
"I was about to hurl my hatchet at his head--
"--and I had a right to do so, for a sailor aboard is master--

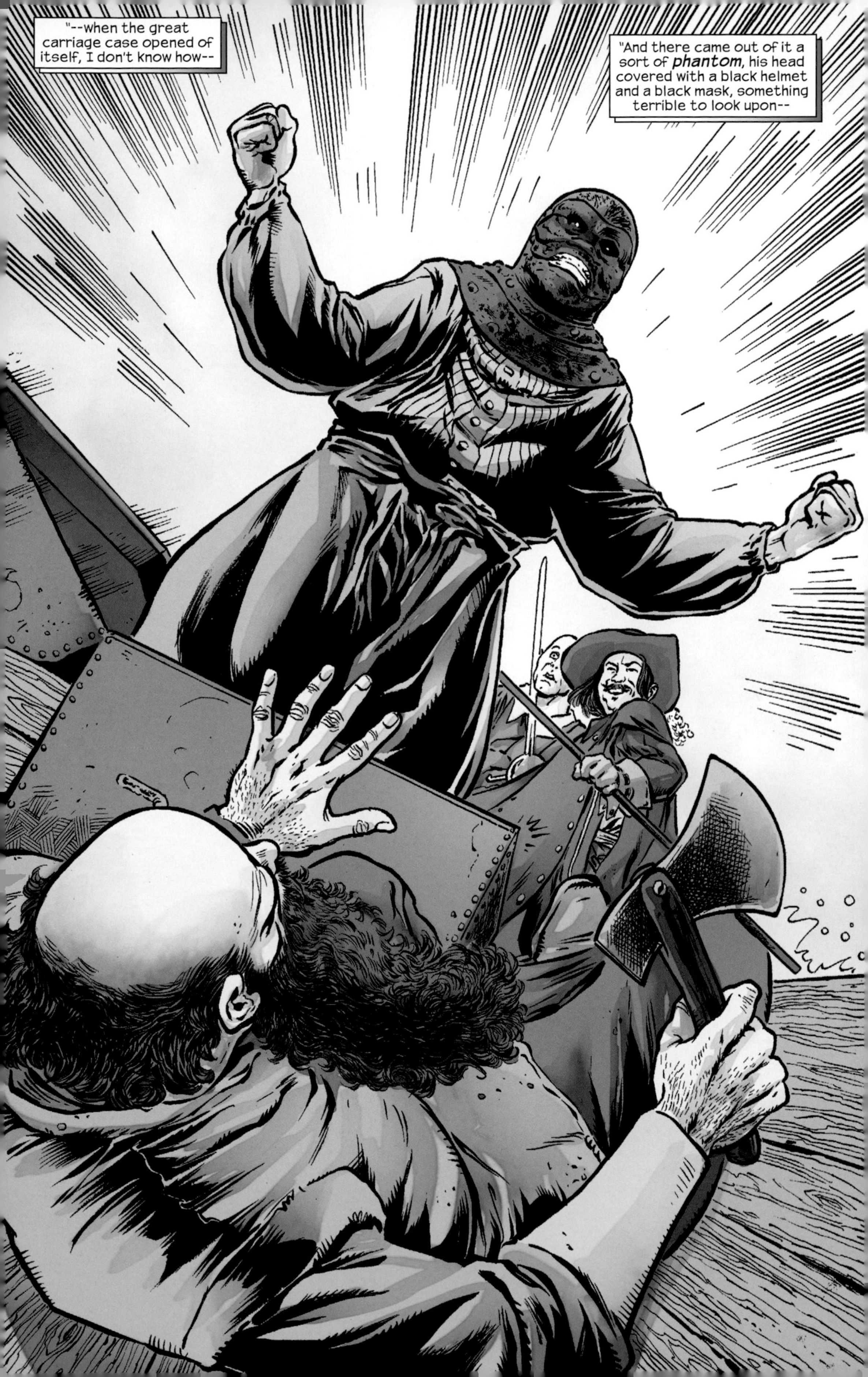
"--when the great carriage case opened of itself, I don't know how--
"And there came out of it a sort of *phantom*, his head covered with a black helmet and a black mask, something terrible to look upon--

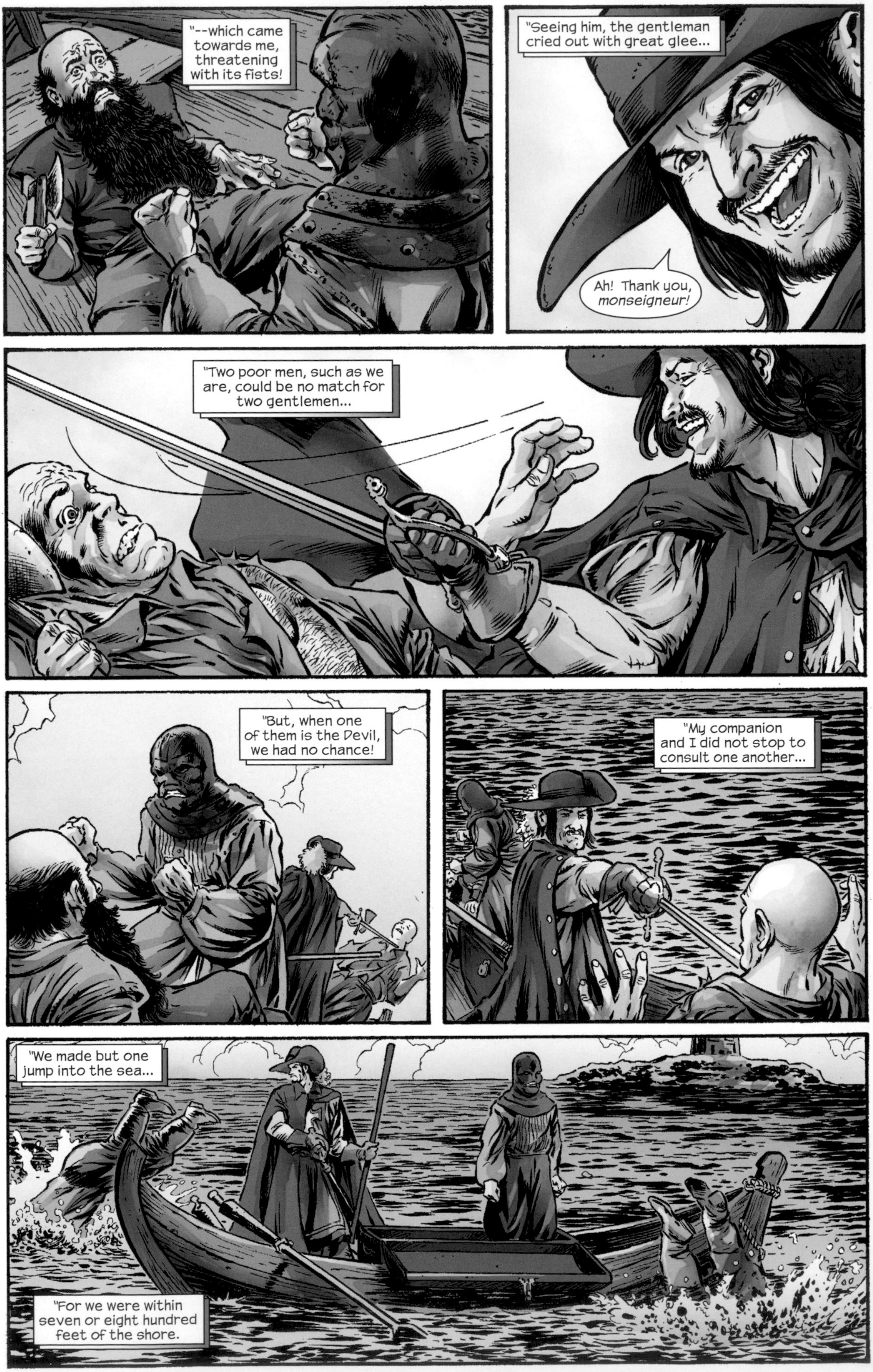
"--which came towards me, threatening with its fists!
"Seeing him, the gentleman cried out with great glee...
Ah! Thank you, *monseigneur!*
"Two poor men, such as we are, could be no match for two gentlemen...
"But, when one of them is the Devil, we had no chance!
"My companion and I did not stop to consult one another...
"We made but one jump into the sea...
"For we were within seven or eight hundred feet of the shore.

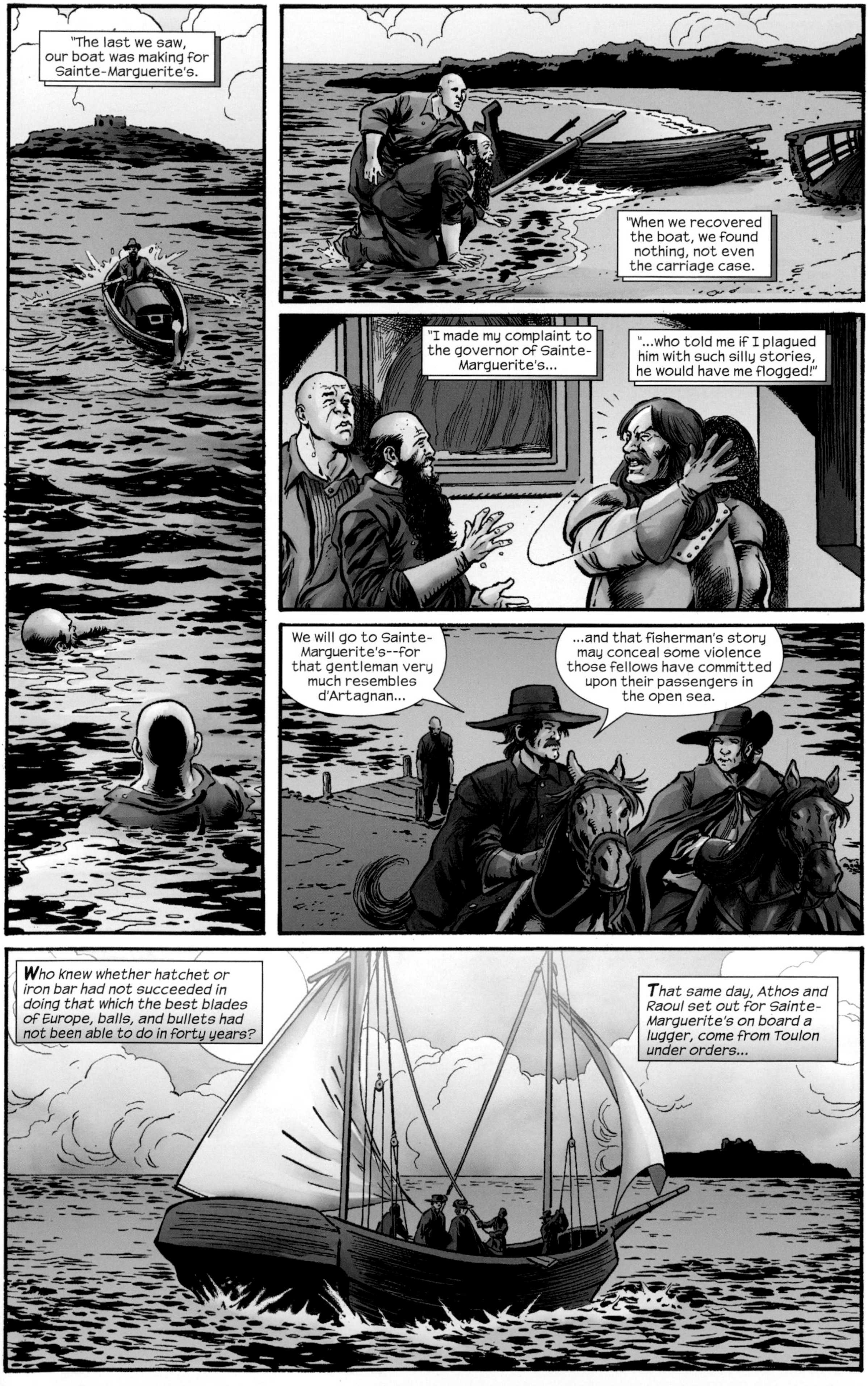
"The last we saw, our boat was making for Sainte-Marguerite's.
"When we recovered the boat, we found nothing, not even the carriage case.
"I made my complaint to the governor of Sainte-Marguerite's...
"...who told me if I plagued him with such silly stories, he would have me flogged!"
We will go to Sainte-Marguerite's--for that gentleman very much resembles d'Artagnan...
...and that fisherman's story may conceal some violence those fellows have committed upon their passengers in the open sea.
Who knew whether hatchet or iron bar had not succeeded in doing that which the best blades of Europe, balls, and bullets had not been able to do in forty years?
That same day, Athos and Raoul set out for Sainte-Marguerite's on board a lugger, come from Toulon under orders...

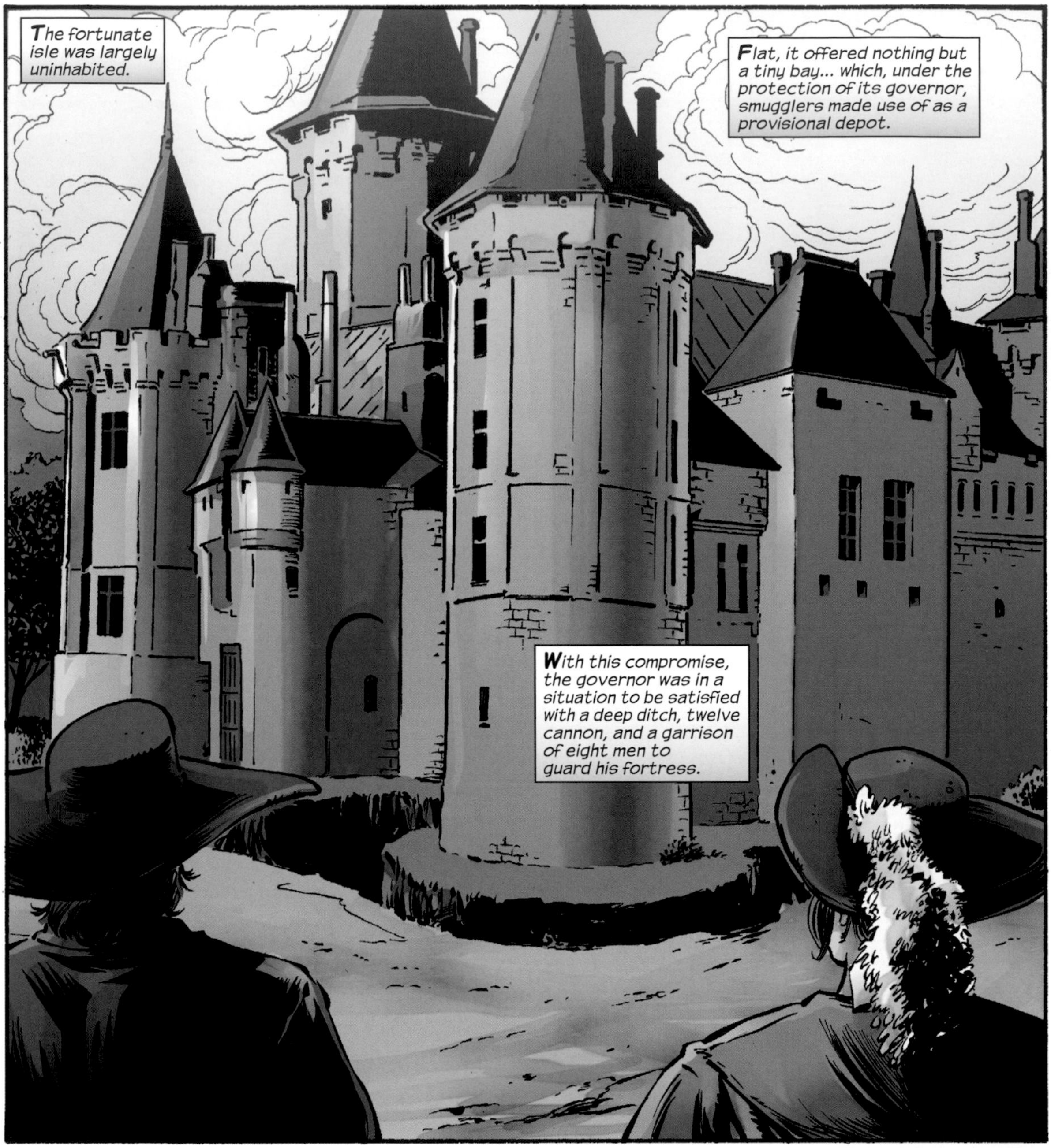
The fortunate isle was largely uninhabited.
Flat, it offered nothing but a tiny bay... which, under the protection of its governor, smugglers made use of as a provisional depot.
With this compromise, the governor was in a situation to be satisfied with a deep ditch, twelve cannon, and a garrison of eight men to guard his fortress.

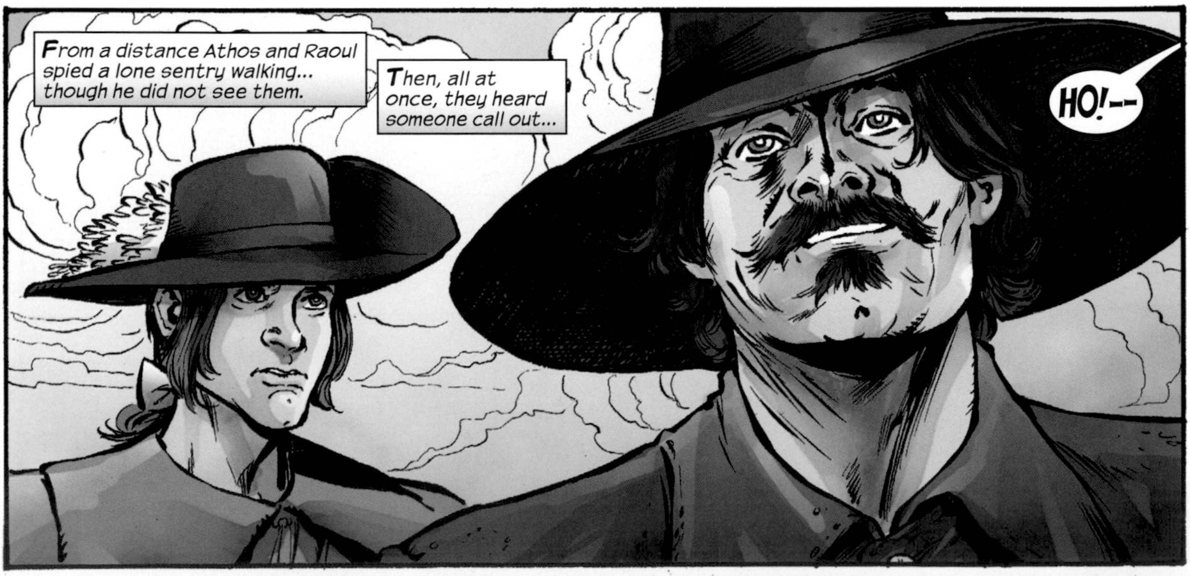
From a distance Athos and Raoul spied a lone sentry walking... though he did not see them.
Then, all at once, they heard someone call out...
HO!--

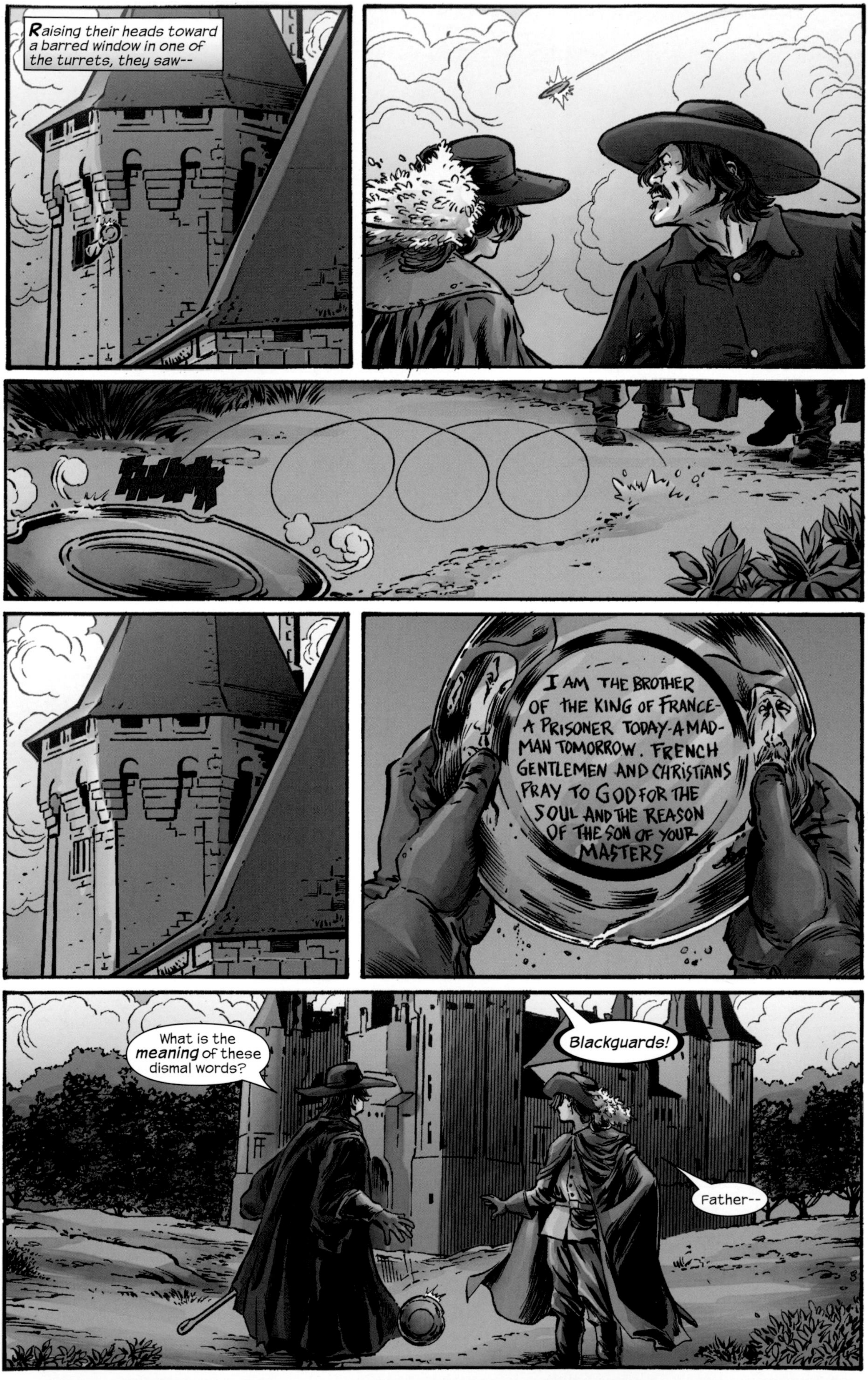
Raising their heads toward a barred window in one of the turrets, they saw--
I AM THE BROTHER OF THE KING OF FRANCE- A PRISONER TODAY-A MADMAN TOMORROW. FRENCH GENTLEMEN AND CHRISTIANS PRAY TO GOD FOR THE SOUL AND THE REASON OF THE SON OF YOUR MASTERS
What is the *meaning* of these dismal words?
Blackguards!
Father--

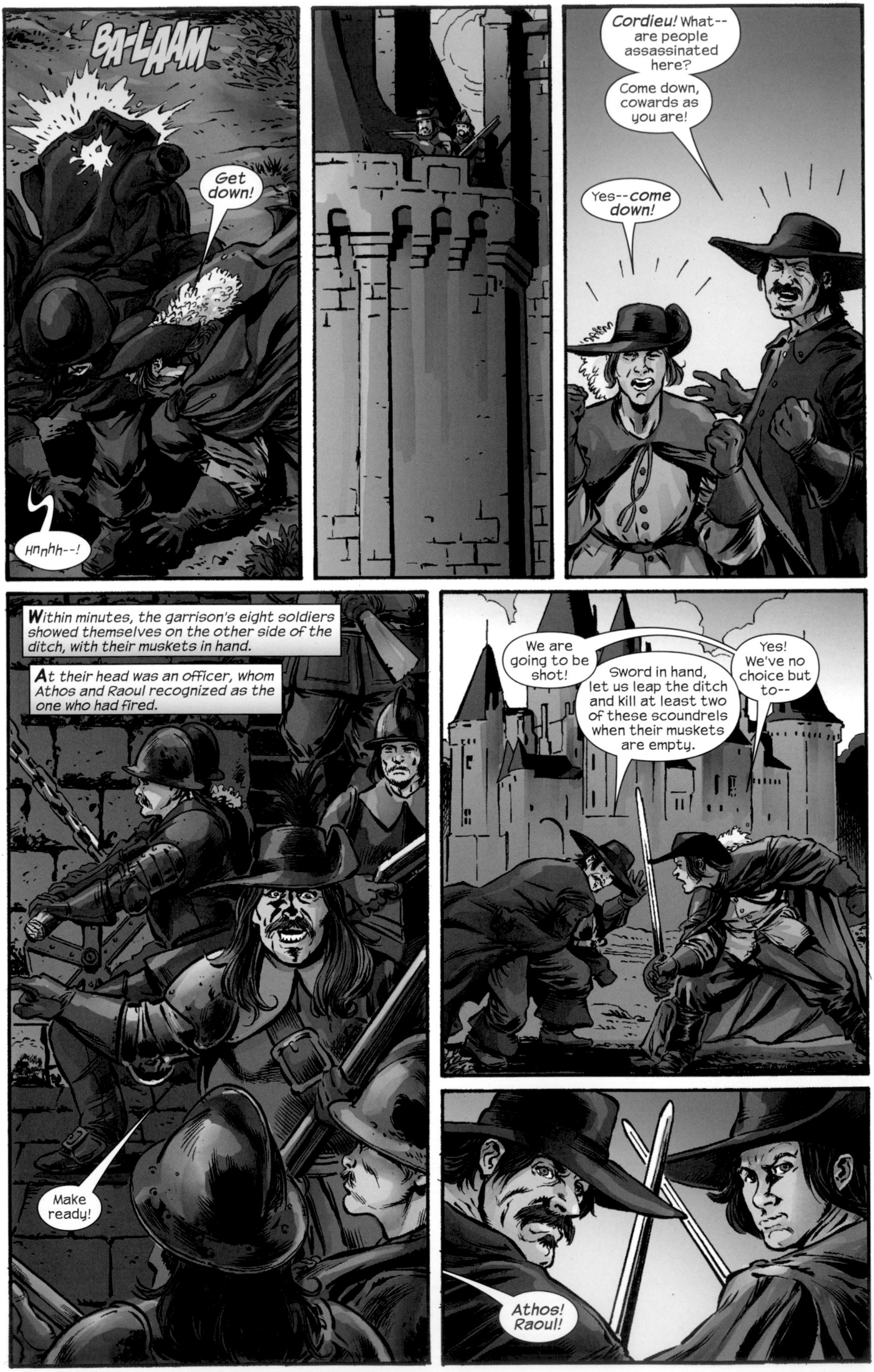
BA-LAAM
Get down!
Hnnhh--!
Cordieu! What-- are people assassinated here?
Come down, cowards as you are!
Yes--come down!
Within minutes, the garrison's eight soldiers showed themselves on the other side of the ditch, with their muskets in hand.
At their head was an officer, whom Athos and Raoul recognized as the one who had fired.
Make ready!
We are going to be shot!
Sword in hand, let us leap the ditch and kill at least two of these scoundrels when their muskets are empty.
Yes! We've no choice but to--
Athos! Raoul!

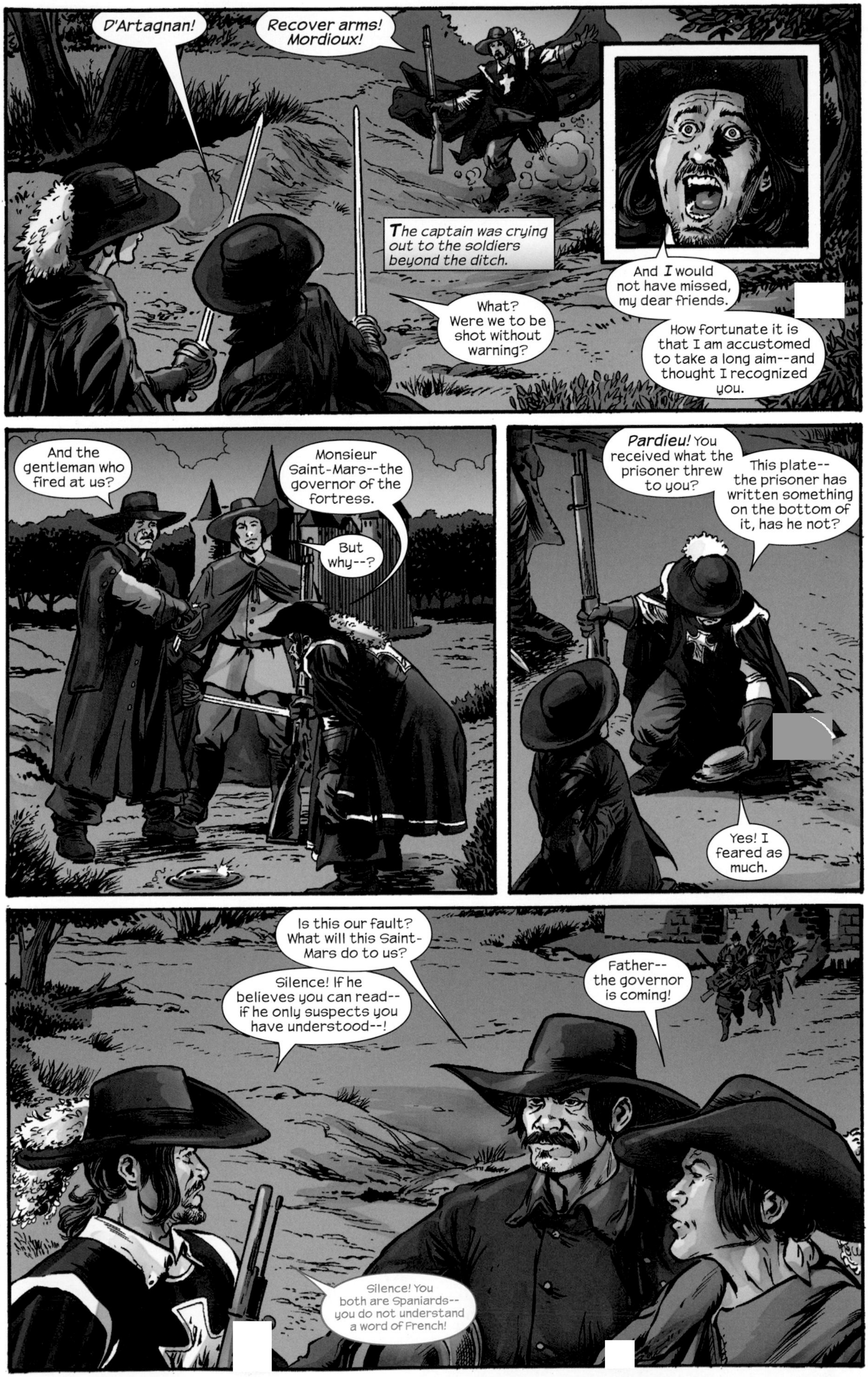
D'Artagnan!
Recover arms! Mordioux!
The captain was crying out to the soldiers beyond the ditch.
What? Were we to be shot without warning?
And I would not have missed, my dear friends.
How fortunate it is that I am accustomed to take a long aim--and thought I recognized you.
And the gentleman who fired at us?
Monsieur Saint-Mars--the governor of the fortress.
But why--?
Pardieu! You received what the prisoner threw to you?
This plate--the prisoner has written something on the bottom of it, has he not?
Yes! I feared as much.
Is this our fault? What will this Saint-Mars do to us?
Silence! If he believes you can read--if he only suspects you have understood--!
Father--the governor is coming!
Silence! You both are Spaniards--you do not understand a word of French!

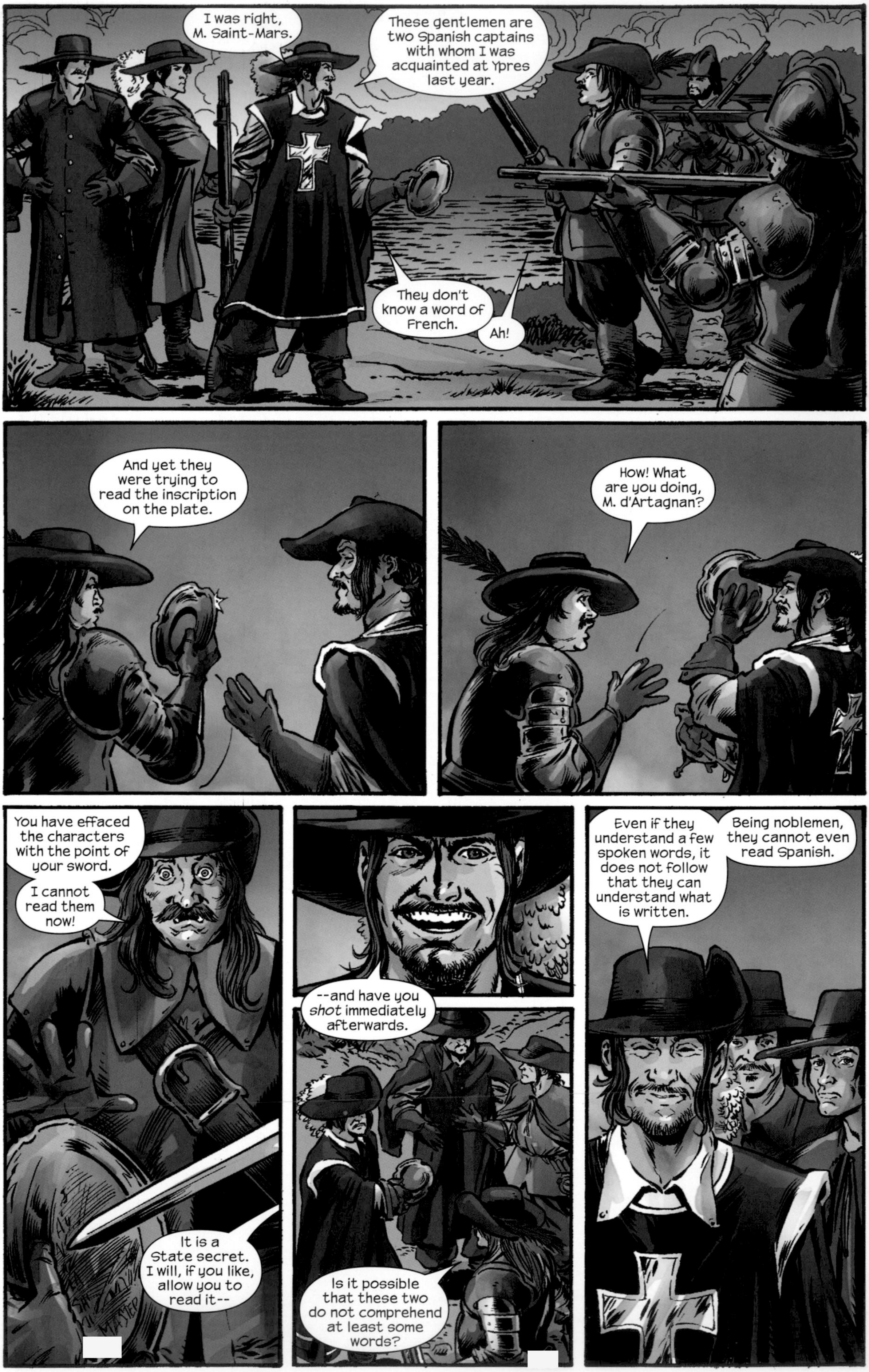
I was right, M. Saint-Mars.
These gentlemen are two Spanish captains with whom I was acquainted at Ypres last year.
They don't know a word of French.
Ah!
And yet they were trying to read the inscription on the plate.
How! What are you doing, M. d'Artagnan?
You have effaced the characters with the point of your sword.
I cannot read them now!
It is a State secret. I will, if you like, allow you to read it--
--and have you *shot* immediately afterwards.
Is it possible that these two do not comprehend at least some words?
Even if they understand a few spoken words, it does not follow that they can understand what is written.
Being noblemen, they cannot even read Spanish.

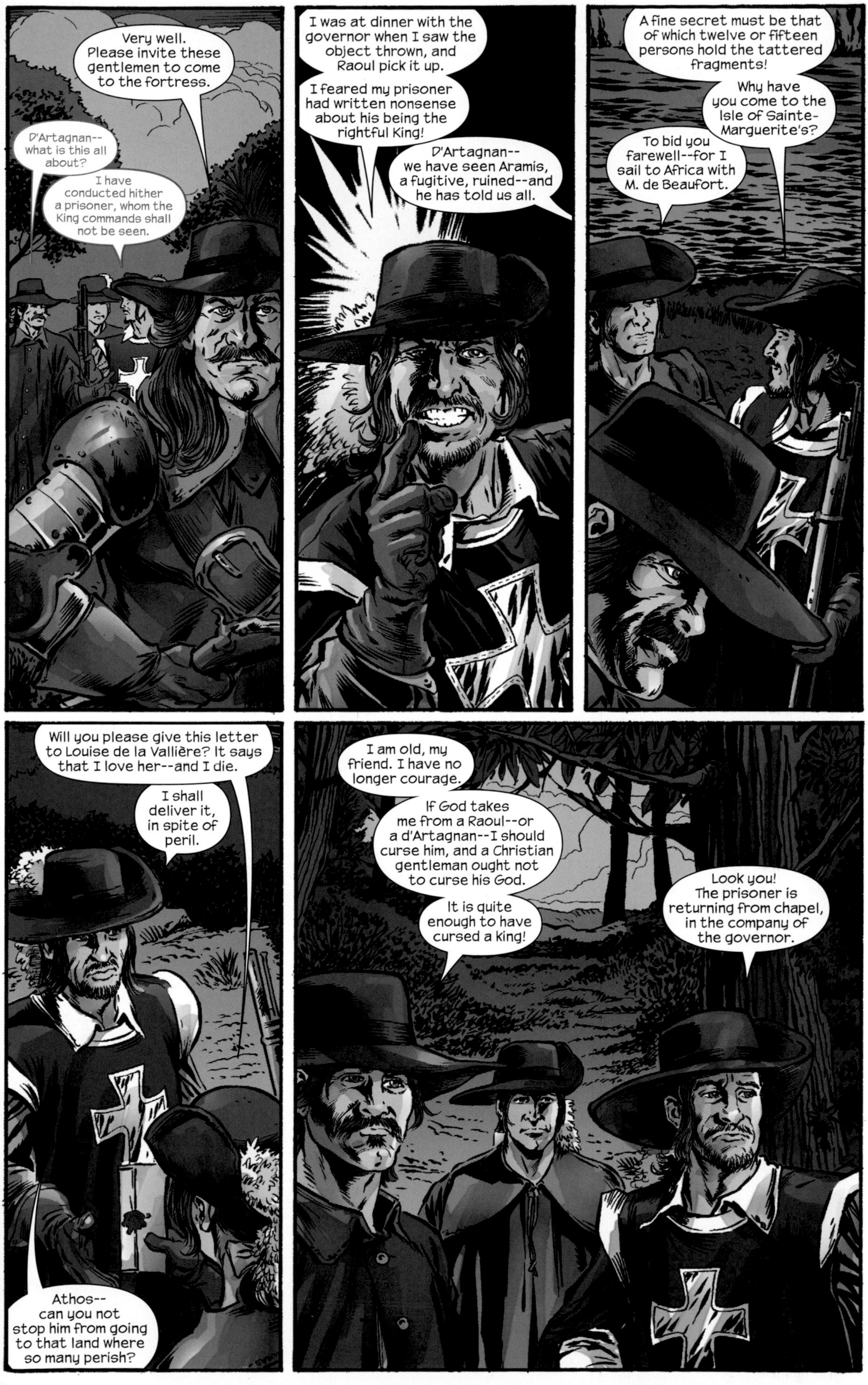

Very well. Please invite these gentlemen to come to the fortress.
D'Artagnan-- what is this all about?
I have conducted hither a prisoner, whom the King commands shall not be seen.
I was at dinner with the governor when I saw the object thrown, and Raoul pick it up.
I feared my prisoner had written nonsense about his being the rightful King!
D'Artagnan-- we have seen Aramis, a fugitive, ruined--and he has told us all.
A fine secret must be that of which twelve or fifteen persons hold the tattered fragments!
Why have you come to the Isle of Sainte-Marguerite's?
To bid you farewell--for I sail to Africa with M. de Beaufort.
Will you please give this letter to Louise de la Vallière? It says that I love her--and I die.
I shall deliver it, in spite of peril.
Athos-- can you not stop him from going to that land where so many perish?
I am old, my friend. I have no longer courage.
If God takes me from a Raoul--or a d'Artagnan--I should curse him, and a Christian gentleman ought not to curse his God.
It is quite enough to have cursed a king!
Look you! The prisoner is returning from chapel, in the company of the governor.

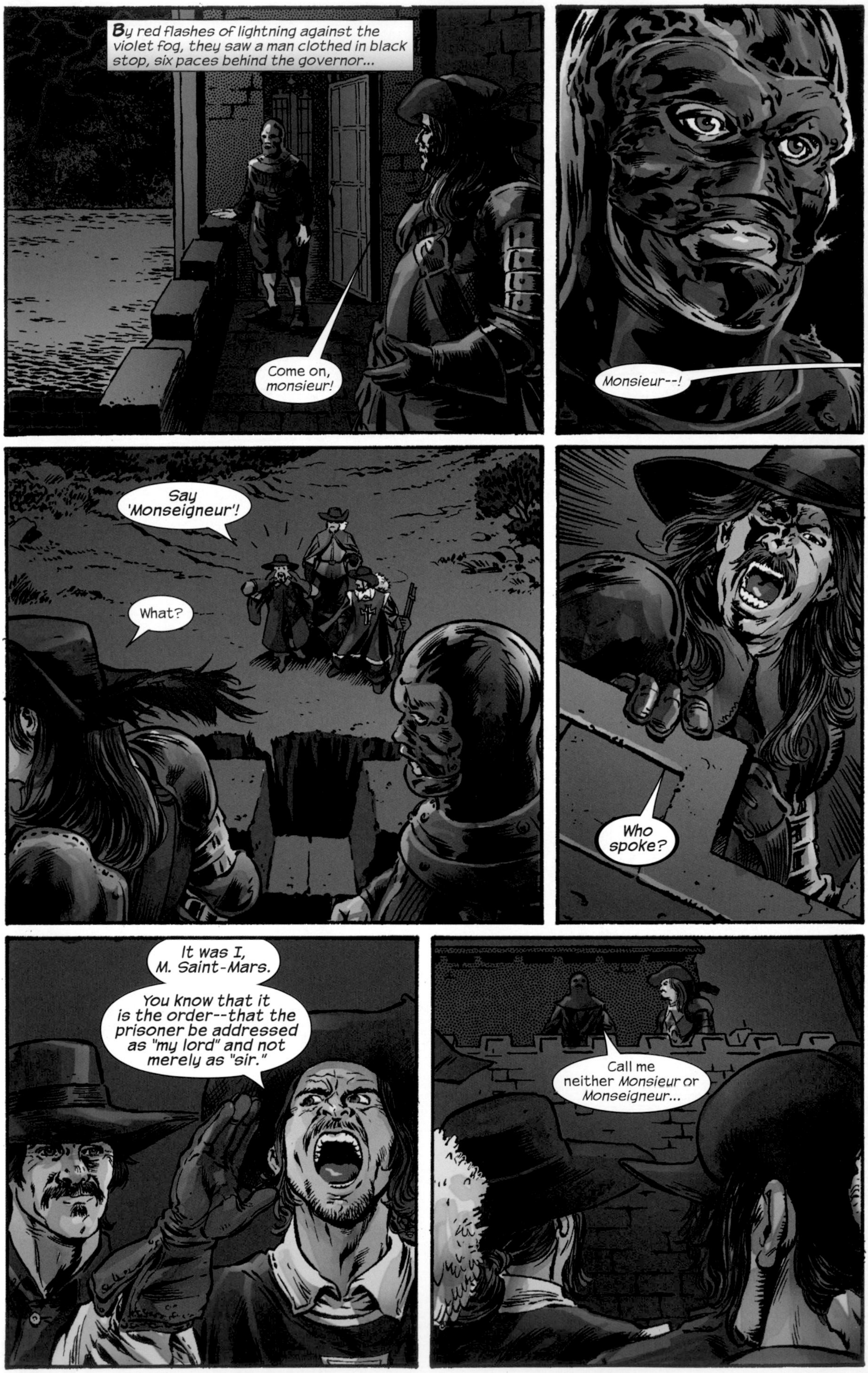

By red flashes of lightning against the violet fog, they saw a man clothed in black stop, six paces behind the governor...
Come on, monsieur!
Monsieur--!
Say 'Monseigneur'!
What?
Who spoke?
It was I, M. Saint-Mars.
You know that it is the order--that the prisoner be addressed as "my lord" and not merely as "sir."
Call me neither *Monsieur* or *Monseigneur*...

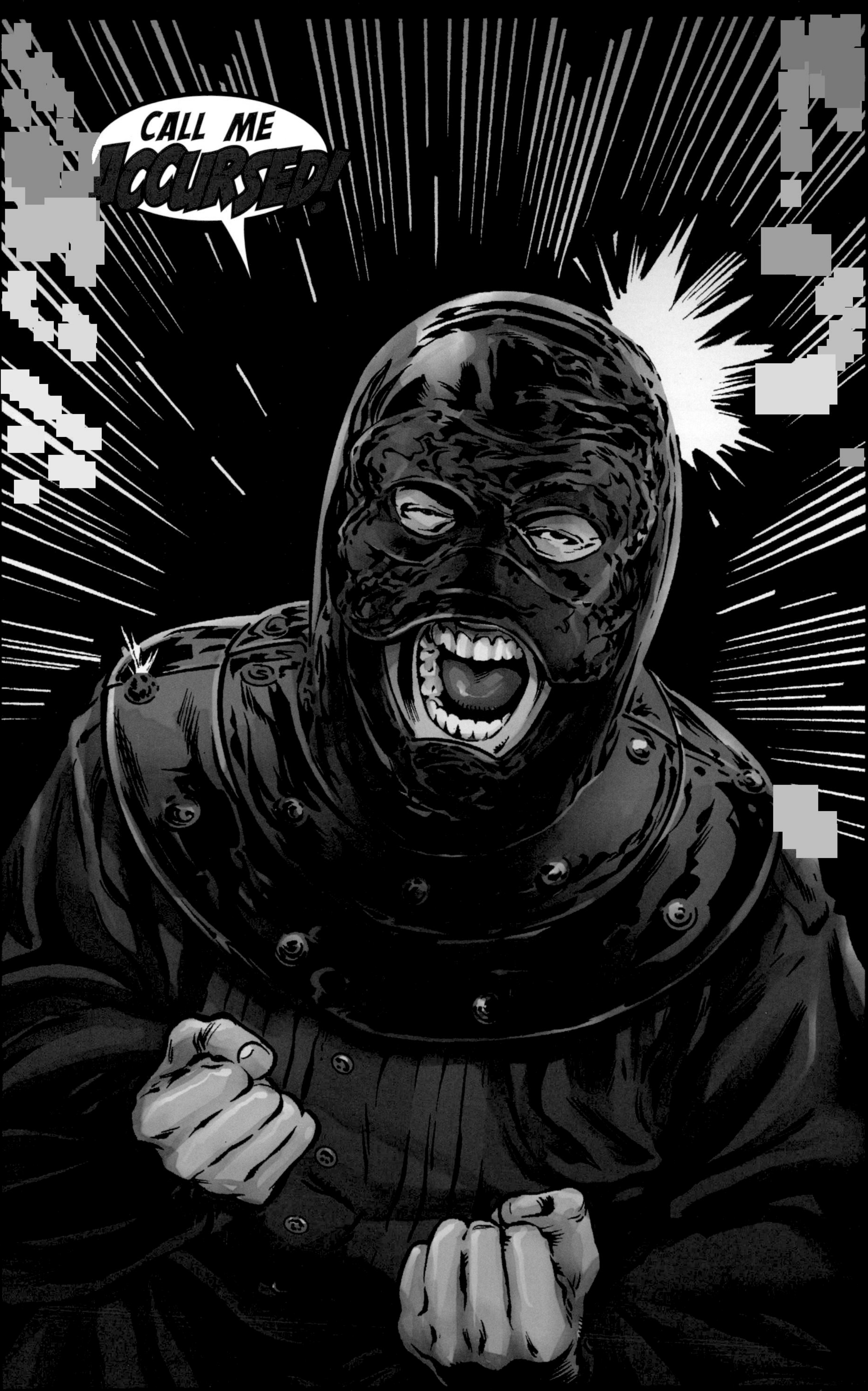
CALL ME ACCURSED!

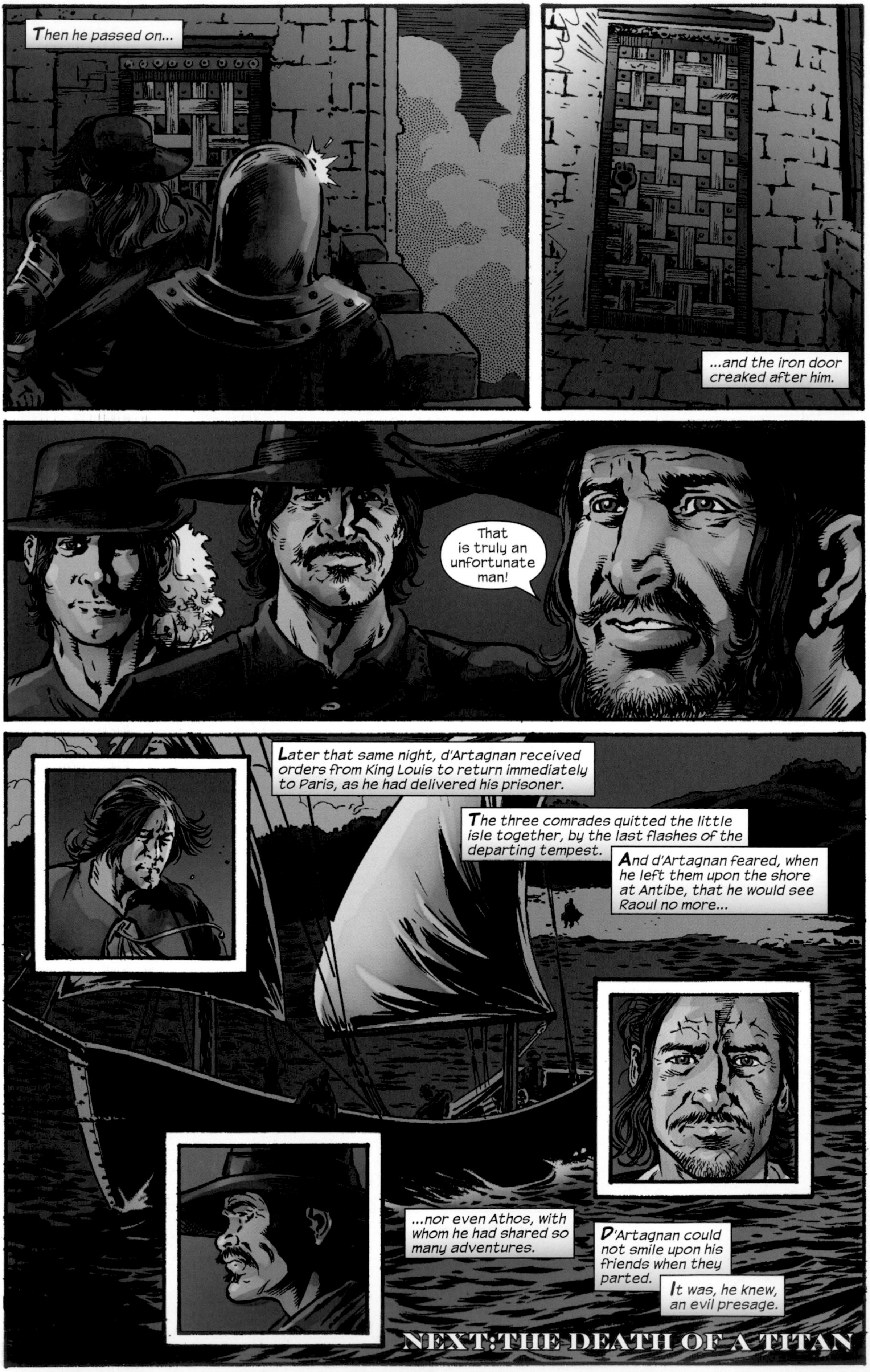
Then he passed on...
...and the iron door creaked after him.
That is truly an unfortunate man!
Later that same night, d'Artagnan received orders from King Louis to return immediately to Paris, as he had delivered his prisoner.
The three comrades quitted the little isle together, by the last flashes of the departing tempest.
And d'Artagnan feared, when he left them upon the shore at Antibe, that he would see Raoul no more...
...nor even Athos, with whom he had shared so many adventures.
D'Artagnan could not smile upon his friends when they parted.
It was, he knew, an evil presage.
NEXT: THE DEATH OF A TITAN